YEAR ONE

2019

Compiled & Edited by
Ben Thomas & D Kershaw

Also available from Black Hare Press

DARK DRABBLES ANTHOLOGIES

WORLDS
ANGELS
MONSTERS
BEYOND
UNRAVEL
APOCALYPSE
LOVE
HATE
OCEANS
ANCIENTS

BHP WRITERS' GROUP SPECIAL EDITIONS

STORMING AREA 51
EERIE CHRISTMAS
BAD ROMANCE

OTHER VOLUMES

DEEP SEA
WHAT IF?
KEY TO THE KINGDOM
BEYOND THE REALM

Twitter: @BlackHarePress
Facebook: BlackHarePress
Website: www.BlackHarePress.com

Year One Anthology title is
Copyright © 2019 Black Hare Press
First published in Australia in December 2019 by Black Hare Press

The authors of the individual stories retain the copyright of the works
featured in this anthology.

*All characters and events in this publication, other than those clearly in the
public domain, are fictitious and any resemblance to real persons, living or
dead, is purely coincidental.*

All rights reserved. No part of this production may be reproduced, stored in
a retrieval system, or transmitted, in any form or by any means, electronic,
mechanical, photocopying, recording or otherwise, without the prior
permission of the publisher and copyright owner.

Paperback : ISBN 978-1-925809-43-5
Hard Cover : ISBN 978-1-925809-44-2

Cover Design by Dawn Burdett
Book Formatting by Ben Thomas

He lieth still: he doth not move:

He will not see the dawn of day.

He hath no other life above.

He gave me a friend and a true truelove

And the New-year will take 'em away.

Old year you must not go;

So long you have been with us,

Such joy as you have seen with us,

Old year, you shall not go.

…

His face is growing sharp and thin.

Alack! our friend is gone,

Close up his eyes: tie up his chin:

Step from the corpse, and let him in

That standeth there alone,

And waiteth at the door.

There's a new foot on the floor, my friend,

And a new face at the door, my friend,

A new face at the door.

The Death of The Old Year **by Alfred Lord Tennyson, 1903**

Table of Contents

Foreword

We set off at the beginning of 2019, fresh-faced into the fiction industry, with just a handful of author acquaintances, and we're ending the year with a whole bunch of new friends!

We're thankful to everyone who came on board with us in those early days and have stayed for the ride, and also to everyone who has joined us on the way. Also, of course, we're thankful of all the new readers who have bought and enjoyed our publications.

We're still learning every day—opening themes, trying new internal styles, finessing—and we hope to keep doing that through next year. Hopefully you'll stick with us for more fiction fun in 2020.

Love and kisses
Ben & Dean

Black Hare Press

FIVE CLUB

At the beginning of 2019, we launched our Dark Drabbles series, starting with the science fiction themed *Worlds*. Each subsequent book had a specific theme and featured around three hundred 100-word tales, with a maximum of five stories per author allowed.

At the end of book 5, we had 24 authors who had managed to get five stories published in each of the first five Dark Drabbles books, and we decided to hold a competition for them. The prize; a coveted MasterClass subscription!

The following are the drabble entries for the final competition.

The winner was Joel R. Hunt with his story *The Dream Merchant*, which we hope you find deserving of the grand prize.

The Dream Merchant

by Joel R. Hunt

The dream merchant couldn't complain; business had never been better. Everyone knew he supplied only the richest and sweetest of dreams.

What fewer customers realised was that stocks had been running low for months. He had started using his own dreams to keep up with demand.

As he refilled the empty storeroom, his daughter ran in with a smile.

"I want to help," said the girl, holding out a glowing sphere. The bright dream of a child.

The merchant cupped his daughter's hands and closed them.

"No," he said, "I only sold my dreams so that you could keep yours."

So You Think You Can Drabble

by Jefferson Retallack

So you think you can drabble.

Don't worry. I get it. You're no amateur writer. The blinking cursor, the blank page, they never last in your presence.

But therein lies the problem. You've wasted twenty-seven words on an intro. And until this line existed, you didn't even have a conflict.

Fifty words now, above this line.

Halfway, oh dear. Stop wasting time.

You've been struggling, scrambling, scrabbling. You'll need to think differently if you want to master drabbling.

Stop the rhyming. Alliteration was never your friend.

But I am.

Just remember one thing: The crux of any good drabble is—

Sunlight and Severance

by Pamela Jeffs

I loved him first.

I loved him best.

Not the wife holding his hand—the hand of my farmer-son, grown sick and paper-thin.

He was my babe. He grew in my light.

As a teenager he toiled under my glaring eye.

Middle-aged—together we watched shades of sunset paint tilled fields.

Years have passed. My son is dying.

But at the end he asks his wife for me.

She brings him out.

I kiss his cheeks. I warm his limbs.

He smiles and then passes.

I weep.

The wife weeps too.

But still I, Mother Sun, loved the farmer best.

The Connoisseur Conundrum

by Umair Mirxa

Gottfried closed his eyes, exhaled, and said a quick prayer. Each new arrival added to the already overwhelming scent of blood inside the hut. Two wounded soldiers he could manage. Twenty made it nearly impossible for him to work.

At sunset, having patched up his latest charge, he stepped outside and lit a cigarette.

"A vampire who would be a nurse," said a voice in his ear. "Have you really stooped so low, brother?"

"No, Dietrich. Not a nurse," Gottfried turned, and smiled at his brother. "Merely a connoisseur. For what would we eat if we let our food perish?"

The Departure

by E.L. Giles

Cradled in his father's arms, the boy opened his eyes weakly. The dim light burned. Moaning, he shut his eyes tightly.

"It hurts, Papa," said the son, his voice barely audible.

"I know," said the father.

Powerless and desperate, he walked across the room and sat by the window, rocking his dying son back and forth, humming his favourite song.

"It's so cold, Papa. I'm afraid."

"Don't be." He laid a blanket on him. "I won't ever leave you, Son."

The father glanced sideways. The shotgun lay nearby against a wall, loaded. He sighed, resolved, relieved.

"I love you, Son."

Taboos

by Vonnie Winslow Crist

Kade the Urisk spied a fairy near his waterfall. Though forbidden to interact with her kind, he stepped closer—his goat-feet clattering on rocks.

"Greetings. I'm Kade."

She stood. Shyly replied, "I'm Dallin."

Thus, their friendship began.

Within days, they were bonded—but their pairing was taboo.

One morning, after deciding to elope, Kade and Dallin joined hands, raced toward the river.

Focused on escape, they paid little attention to danger. An ogre—with no taboos—spotted, caught, then ate them both.

Weeks later, Meadow Fairies and Urisks found a pile of Kade's and Dallin's bones: in death, together forever.

Wingreen Reprise

by C.L. Williams

A suicide pact with a priest gone rogue. A family thinking, they were following the path to immortality. Only, a change of heart occurred from the priest upon the announcement that he is a father to be. An aristocratic family now living on Earth as ghosts because of a miscommunication from the man they once believed to be their leader.

A father now ready to take the reigns as leader of the group he once called his home and a family hellbent on revenge. First, they must keep the family large, then seek vengeance on the father that abandoned them.

One Submission Call to Rule Them All

by Shelly Jarvis

Ben watched Bree's ship hovering above the station, waiting for the grav-beam to draw it into the hangar. He threw a nutrition pod in the expander and waited. Bree entered the lab, stretching her limbs in eight directions.

"Rough day?" he asked, handing her a pod.

"These again?"

Ben nodded. "Until we figure out how to harness the Earthling minds."

Dean-bot rolled into the room, chirping excitedly. Understanding crossed their frontal lobes in unison. She asked, "Will it work?"

Ben shrugged two of his shoulders. "Dean-bot thinks so." He patted Dean-bot's cylindrical top, saying, "Very well. Tomorrow, we'll open submissions."

The Best Ever

by Stephen Herczeg

His mind was aflame. Electricity arced through his brain, racing across every synapse, setting his neurons on fire.

He felt possessed. As if his soul had been offered to a demon who speared it with deadly fangs and happily munched away, feeding his intellect with the untold knowledge of aeons.

His fingers flashed away, dancing a frantic tarantella, a blurring flurry of movement before him.

His eyes watered, absorbing what formed before them.

Tears materialised at their corners and ran as he perused what had been presented.

In all the years of toil.

This was the best he'd ever written.

Ad Break

by David Bowmore

"No one expected the Zombie Apocalypse."

"Who are you? The lost member of Monty Python?"

"I'm serious. Human genes are mutating. As a species, we're done for."

"What particular comic did you read this in?"

"The New Alchemist. Before long we'll all be mindless zombies with a constant hunger for human flesh."

"Bollocks!"

"It's true. They found this bloke in America without a will of his own, and apparently dead. He wasn't breathing, had no heartbeat, and couldn't feel anything, but was still walking around looking for brains."

"That'll be their president. Now, be quiet and let me watch this."

Fresh Blood

by Dawn DeBraal

Ordering their favourite cocktails, Barnabus and Vladimir took a seat at the bar.

"Anemia and Last Drop," the bartender said as he placed their drinks in front of them.

At the sound of a gasp, the publican quickly disconnected the hose attached to a donor marked "Last Drop," hauling him into the back room. "Anemia" was then moved to the "Last Drop" position, while "Fresh Blood" was moved to "Anemia's" spot. The friends wondered where the bartender would get a replacement for the newly vacated spot. A new guy walked into the bar.

"Hey! Fresh Blood!" called out the patrons.

Suspension

by Terry Miller

"Loneliness isn't forever. Eventually, we all die."

It wasn't the pep talk Jordan was hoping to hear. The spirit faded into the mist as Jordan fought back the tears. If he pulled the trigger, it was over; if he didn't, tomorrow would be the same. She didn't love him, she never did. He knew that now. The back of Jordan's head exploded with blood and brains plastered to the tree behind him.

"I told you we all die," the spirit reminded him. "But I lied about the loneliness."

The spirit again disappeared into nothingness, Jordan's soul suspended in the same.

Dinner Party

by Sinister Sweetheart

I learned that my neighbour was vegan and figured I'd give it a try. It sounded like an amazing way to cleanse your body while building self-discipline. I was promptly invited to a dinner party.

Sitting down to eat, they announced they had a secret. They told me they were vegan cannibals.

Shocked, I asked them how such a thing was possible.

Our neighbour flicked a smile my way and replied, "Easy…we only eat Vegans."

My eyelids became heavy. The last thing I saw in my fleeting moments of consciousness, was their carpet turning crimson after I hit the floor.

Bloody Correction

by Alexander Pyles

There was a single set of footsteps, red, on the linoleum. You don't know what to think. You only follow the trail down the hallway. A knife held tightly to your side. It's quiet, except for a wet tearing sound.

You find her. Her hospital gown torn, viscera staining the front. Her hair is draped over her eyes, but you already know who they are. She isn't breathing, but her body stirs and turns from the meal.

This is why you are here. A cure gone wrong and guilt.

She lunges and you lead with the sharp edge and regret.

Even Death May Die

by Raven Corinn Carluk

The stars were right.

"Ia! Ie!" The cultists cheered, abandoning their shadowed cellars and hidden lairs. Deep Ones rose from murky waters, swarming into ports and through unprepared cities. Humans ran and screamed, unable to comprehend the dark tidings.

Madness spread like a plague, bringing chaos and panic with it. People tore themselves apart, killing strangers in the streets, even slaughtering their own families.

Cthulhu rolled over, shaking the walls of R'lyeh with his movements. He yawned deeply, reality echoing with the sound, and he pressed snooze on the cosmic clock.

The stars would still be right in ten minutes.

Life's Simple Pleasures

by Eddie D. Moore

A rapturous shiver ran down Dean's spine and goosebumps peppered his flesh as he leaned back in his chair. The cool air of the basement and the metallic smell of blood created the perfect setting for the dark tasks at hand. Fingernails littered the floor, and wet pieces of meat clung to hooks hanging from the ceiling joists. A smile tugged at Dean's lips as his eyes flicked over the gory remains of his victims.

He said softly, "Oh, life's simple pleasures," and turned back to his computer. The exhilarating chills returned as he typed: Unfortunately, your story has not…

Innocence Lost

by Zoey Xolton

Each night the monster comes into my room. My skin crawls and my insides shrivel inside me—knowing there is no escape. The darkness is traitorously thin. *It can't hide me.*

I lie, paralysed by fear as the door inches open, clicking shut shortly after. I hear the heavy, tell-tale breathing; smell the acrid stench of stale cigarette smoke.

I clutch the covers and press myself to the wall, but it doesn't help. The covers are pulled back and sweaty hands reach out—the monster's hot breath washes over me.

I pray for help, but God never seems to hear.

Wake

by G. Allen Wilbanks

He awoke, reaching across the bed but finding only empty sheets. The smell of coffee brewing tickled his nose, bringing a small smile to his lips.

He rose, head foggy from sleep, and staggered out to the kitchen.

"Morning, hon. When did you…?"

The kitchen was empty.

Suddenly, viciously, the memories came flooding back: The scream of rending metal. Flashing red and blue lights. The funeral a week later.

He crawled back into bed, burrowing into the covers and closing his eyes tight. He sought the blessed oblivion of sleep.

Maybe this time he would finally wake from the nightmare.

Rip Off Bandage

by Shawn M. Klimek

"But our wedding date is set, and it takes six weeks to heal from a rhinoplasty," Franklin whined. "They break your nose, you know."

"I love you, Frank, but I could never marry a snoring, mouth-breather!" Kendra insisted.

Fortunately, Franklin's humour put the wedding guests at ease about his bandaged face. Likewise, his self-deprecating wit coupled with a doctor's note and horrific wedding photos tickled the Cancún customs agent.

At the honeymoon's conclusion, that same agent laughed to see him still bandaged.

"Adios, Señor y Señora Mummy!" he joked, as he stamped their passports.

"Adios," said Kendra.

Carlos stayed mum.

No Vengeance for Eleanor

by Aiki Flinthart

In bitterest winter, Eleanor returns to the gilded halls of my inheritance.

My elder sister's icy whisper caresses my heated cheek. "I am murdered," says a tongue I thought long-rotted in her dirt-muffled mouth. A tongue telling truths enough to free our father from his ensorcelled eyrie. Our mother from her tear-drowned, black oubliette.

"By who? There was no proof." A held breath lies heavy in my chest. "Be at peace."

"Unavenged, I cannot rest easy." Eleanor's fierce sorrow rends my heart, my hopes.

"I can't help you."

"Then I'll stay by my killer."

I flee, Eleanor at my side.

The Kid-napper

by Stuart Conover

Josh never thought that he would be a kid-napper.

Yet when properly motivated, he'd do anything.

They knew just how to manipulate him.

No one really believed that it was a Satanic cult that lived at the edge of town.

Now he knew better.

The authorities didn't seem to believe him that they had taken Stacey.

It didn't make sense, until the Sheriff pulled him aside and revealed the truth.

He was part of it.

They needed his access to the kids.

She'd go free with his help.

Because of this, Josh ended up here.

Surrounded by thirteen baby goats.

What Lies in the Darkness

by Crystal L. Kirkham

I lay awake and long for sleep. The darkness screams for my attention.

My pulse races, terror claws at my mind. I know what waits for me.

Unable to resist, I look towards the ceiling.

Eyes stare back at me, gleaming with madness.

The world shudders and she falls. I shield my face as she slams into me, shattering into a million pieces.

Everything stills.

My door slams open. Light assaults my eyes, reflecting off the shards of mirror surrounding me. I'm covered in cuts, but alive.

My mother cries, happy I'm alright.

I wish I could feel the same.

Bountiful Harvest

by John H. Dromey

Representatives of Terran colonists on a remote planet eagerly signed a multibillion-credits contract offered by an alien race for mineral rights in perpetuity.

The chief negotiator was curious. "This planet's resources are nearly depleted. What's your interest? A rare element found so far beneath the surface our miners were unable to extract it?"

"Nothing that exotic."

"What then?"

"A straightforward extraction of easily accessible minerals. Your omission of a protection clause for indigenous lifeforms was a serious oversight on your part. The human body contains significant or trace amounts of many minerals. Calcium, phosphorus, potassium, sodium, magnesium, zinc, and so on."

Flashback

by Cecelia Hopkins-Drewer

It was a flashback, she was sure. Hazy and murky. An elongated, segmented body and multiple legs. Almost as big as a horse. She was not frightened; she was petting something. Something that hummed and twittered.

It was a flashback she was sure. Feeding something. It's mandibles tickling as it accepted the food. Stroking the bullet shaped head. The man came in an astronaut suit. Shouted in alarm and laser beamed her pet. Took Evie away from her planet.

It was a flashback she was sure. Evie was learning things at school, but she missed her old way of life.

BLACK HARE PRESS

YEAR ONE

DARK MOMENTS

Expire

by Alex Gounaris

I floated in space, heading for an endless journey through the darkness until I reached my end, my demise.

My suit kept me warm, but I felt so cold. I panted; the only sound, forever.

Everything was dark except for the KB-11 star in the distance, at the edge of the universe. My last sunset.

The debris of my spaceship passed by slowly. Fragments of my old life.

I tried to grab something and hold onto it, but everything was just out of reach. Like my future.

I closed my eyes tightly and prayed for a miracle.

It didn't come.

A Breath So Sweet

by Stephen Coghlan

Oh, the horror!

I must escape!

I must flee!

But sanctuary is so impossibly far.

I gag!

I gasp!

I weep!

It is brimstone; it is cadavers; it is lethal gasses and deadly pollutants.

Hands claw at my throat, tear at my mask to no avail.

Can I not travel faster?

The airlock grows so slowly through the mist.

It burns, I blink away the pain, but my eyes refuse to focus.

There, numb fingers open the hatch, I crawl inside.

Watch the light.

Wait for it to turn green.

Rip off my helmet.

.

Advice: Never fart in your spacesuit.

Nodes and Modes

by Beth W. Patterson

There was no sound in space, but she felt the music of the spheres with her whole body.

The starship had been programmed with pre-recorded songs to break the tedium. But she pined for live music, even more than she missed green grass beneath her feet, a crisp breeze, or sunlight.

And now looking at this newly discovered solar system, she observed planets in orbit forming intervals and chords as they passed one another. She saw harmony in relativity and motion.

How to begin the song? It will be in the key of whatever world she chooses to land on.

Protected Class

by Adam S. Furman

To the citizens and subjects of the Interplanetary Commonwealth:

Because of the abundance of knowledge about the human mind and great strides made in the understandings thereof, the Ministry of Offense has decided to update its Offense Code. It does hereby recognise individuals identified as IQ-fluid as a protected class. Any discrimination or harassment of an individual that displays any so-called insufficient knowledge, including but not limited to grammar, spelling, or comprehension, will be met with the same punishment as petty theft under £500.

This decree is effective at the moment your transmission is received.

Regards,

Minster of a Fence

The 97-Year-Old Science-Fiction Writer's Untimely Time-Machine Computer

by J.J. Steinfeld

The 97-year-old science-fiction writer began to type the final paragraph of his latest novel. In mid-sentence, a distinguished-looking gentleman appeared on the computer-monitor, replacing text.

"What the hell?" the writer growled.

"Greetings," the monitor-gentleman replied.

"Who are you?"

"Herbert."

"I don't know any damn Herbert."

"I travelled all this way to help."

"Get lost!"

"I know about these things."

"What things?"

"Time travel and writing…"

YEAR ONE

With his last breaths, the writer fought to get the intruder off his computer-monitor. H.G. Wells shook his head mournfully, saying he should have arrived earlier, but had been having trouble mastering electronic time-travel.

First published in Drabble Harvest #7

On the House

by Colleen Anderson

Jordan hated everything; wife left him for goddam grooming parlour, boss said he wasn't meeting his quota.

He'd show them quota. He stormed into a bar, each person's face hidden in the sins of their past.

"Keep 'em coming," he ordered, slapping down his credit card. He would join the sinners.

The bartender snorted. "One rule. Don't pass out. Never pass out!"

Jordan flooded his pain with whiskey shots and beer; then someone with too white a grin bought more.

Severe abdominal pain woke him. Straps restrained him, tubes leading to the bar.

The bartender smiled. "You're on the house."

Quick Salvage

by Eddie D. Moore

I found the derelict in a degrading orbit around the fourth planet. With more time, I might've salvaged the experimental craft, but the computer gave me a forty-five minute window before it plunged into the atmosphere.

Smears of blood decorated the walls, and I tried not to look directly at the disfigured piles of flesh I stepped over to reach the bridge. I uploaded the memory core and grabbed what tech I could on the way out, while mentally tallying up the payout.

Safely aboard my own ship, I was watching the security video when something moved under my skin.

The Hot Bunk

by Shawn M. Klimek

Lieutenant Kent ached. His leaden eyelids fluttered as he struggled to focus on the faces above him.

"How are you feeling, Lieutenant?" asked Doctor Horn.

"Dying," Kent croaked.

"The symbiote is weakening, too," said Horn. "Both of you are dangerously sleep deprived."

"The symbiote has been communicating with us every night!" enthused Major Owens. "It has finally agreed to share Vancian technology!"

"They can't both continue sharing the same body," the doctor clarified.

"But this is a great opportunity for mankind!" pleaded Owens.

"Please," said Kent, fading. "End this!"

"You heard him, Doctor," said the major. "We have his consent."

The Rich, the Poor, and When Earth's Time Is Up

by Aditya Deshmukh

An ashamed sun drags itself up the smoky horizon.

Humongous spaceships, built only for the rich, are leaving. The rich ones, the bright ones, the so-called pillars of the society, are leaving.

Their companies, their negligence, their money is what turned Earth into this foul breath, this disease, this nauseating smell of my father's diarrhoeic stools. The air is black, the rain is acid, my neighbourhood is a graveyard because of them.

And yet they get to leave!

No, I cannot let this happen. I'll unite my people. I'll burn their spaceships. They'll know the power of the working class!

It's So Dark

by Stephen Herczeg

I wake. It's dark. So dark.

My bed is tight. Snug on both sides. I reach up. There's something a few inches above me. It's hard, but covered in soft fabric. It's like I'm in a box, with soft silk sheets all around. I'm wearing a suit, not pyjamas. Where are my shoes?

I'm falling. Slowly. Very slowly. I land with a thump. My bed is jostled, but I can't fall out.

Something lands on top of the box, thud. Then even more thuds. I scream but I have no voice.

Then there's only silence. I'm alone.

It's so dark.

Learn

by Belinda Brady

"Shapeshifters? Why are you reading about them? They're not real," my childhood friend, Joshua, scoffs.

"You know me. I'm always learning something new," I reply, glancing at the book on my table.

Like how I had learned Joshua was sleeping with my wife. That was new.

"You learn about dumb stuff, man," Joshua laughs, getting a beer from the fridge.

The bottle shatters to the floor when he turns around and faces himself.

"You could learn a thing or two, man. Like how to stay away from a friend's wife," I seethe, lunging forward.

I never did get a reply.

Ghulskelche

by Russell Hemmell

"Welcome to The Morgue. At 5 pm, we serve tea. In the evening, different drinks."

Kelly glanced at the barmaid. The nightclub, hosted in a deconsecrated church, was freezing cold, but the girl, ghastly pale with naked shoulders, seemed unaffected.

"It's midnight now."

"And that's champagne o'clock, sweety."

The girl poured and Kelly took a sip. It tasted like champagne, bubbles and everything. Only the colour wasn't right. Carmine red.

"Where?"

"In Hell."

The barmaid's face became opalescent, her eyes glaring white. The flute morphed into a snarling serpent, fangs plunging into Kelly's wrist, blood-like tears on its snout.

Soul Food

by Mike Murphy

The eternal soul fluttered about the bedroom, waiting for instructions either to return to Heaven or the dying man. Joel's family clustered around his bed, the lights from the blinking monitors casting off-and-on red shadows on their faces.

Finally, the soul got its orders and began the careful descent to its host. Seconds later, Gravy, with her incredible feline sight, pounced on it – snatching it from the air and pinning it down.

Joel's blue-haired mother cried out as the heart monitor went flat. In a dark corner, the orange tabby ate happily, knowing she would soon have nine lives again.

They Hang

by John Saxton

They hang; some in bunches, others alone. Umbilical cords connect to maternal branches. The progeny sway in the breeze. Sun bakes the forest floor.

Footsteps! In soft grass. The man salivates, eyes glazed. Pauses; inhales; snarls through discoloured teeth. Bloodshot eyes swivel toward a succulent hatchling. Unsheathes his knife.

The scions sense danger. Scream. Agonisingly.

He falls to his knees, knife dropped. Ears covered, bleeding through fingers.

Foetal leeches jump, cords elastic. Countless needled jaws affix. His death is slow torture. They drain him. Withdraw. Bloated. His alabaster corpse stinks in the calescent sun.

They hang.

Until the next feed.

What Squirms Beneath

by Paul Alex Gray

Chunks of muck splattered Ernie as he blasted the fatberg with his hose.

"Bloody idiots," he grumbled. "Flushing leftovers and nappies and God knows what down the drain. Here I am, swimming in it!"

He aimed the spray at a stubborn glob that hung from the sewer walls, smiling with a grim satisfaction as it peeled away. Unravelling, it drew itself up, a squirming snake of glistening fat.

"What the-?" said Ernie incredulously, dropping the hose.

The putrid fatberg lashed out, a revolting maw of muck wrapping around Ernie's face, suffocating him as it forced its way down his throat.

Grandma's Gift

by J.D. Bell

Weathered hands work the long braid of the witch's ladder with deft skill.

"My dear grandmother taught me how to use this ladder." Gnarled fingers tied the first of several knots.

"And her grandmother taught her of its magical powers." The woman's granddaughter studied the pattern.

"Now, I'm teaching you, Lucy." The woman gave the ladder to Lucy.

"You must concentrate on your intention, wish very hard, and tie the final knot."

Lucy focused her energy on the ladder, then tied the last knot. Moments later, the man who kicked Lucy's dog tumbled down his cellar stairs, breaking both legs.

Excalibur's Prelude

by Dave Ring

Emrys and Fatou le Fay had been practicing their lines in this damn cave for hours. Their first mission: find the stone, swap the swords, get out.

"Stop fussing with the hilt, Fatou."

"It doesn't look right."

"No one's going to notice. They're going to be busy laughing at me for saying thee instead of thou."

A brutal gust of wind snuffed out the candles.

Something growled in the darkness.

"Was that your stomach?" Emrys asked.

Fatou drew her sword. "No."

The beast pounced on Emrys. The transponder crystal shattered beneath her.

"Shit."

Getting out just got a lot harder.

The Butcher of Redcreek Farm

by Zoey Xolton

Jacob shivered in the cage, naked as the day he was born. He curled into a foetal position for warmth. The hay on which he lay pricked and irritated him. His eyes flitted around the slaughter shed. Cages lined the opposite wall, tear streaked faces peered out from each.

In walked The Butcher. His bloody apron flapped as he walked, machete in hand. Jacob closed his eyes and prayed. He felt a sting in his rear and then blissful numbness. The world turned upside down, and then warmth spilled over his face to pool on the cold concrete floor below.

Lady in White

by A.R. Johnston

I slowly walked toward the river, fireflies dancing in front of me. The magic on the air—it was almost tangible. I loved it and I wanted more.

The moon reflected off the river as I approached, the mist rose from it. I watched as the mist started to take form. I was spellbound as a woman in a white dress came to be. The most gorgeous figure I had ever seen.

I knew things would never be the same. I smiled, she smiled back holding her hand in offering. She was a signal of death. Mine was upon me.

Singer

by Steven Sheil

She fell backwards into the crowd and felt their hands take her weight. Sweat-slick fingers pressed into her body as the strobe-light jittered across their faces in time with the pulse of the snare drum. She sucked in a breath as the last line of the song began its journey to her lips, the final animal howl of release, the pinprick that would pierce the membrane of the moment she had created.

It never came, stayed caught instead in the sinews of her throat, as the grasping hands pulled her flesh to wet pieces and their mouths fell to devouring.

O Fear and Fortuna

by L.P. Melling

They rained from the sky, shaped like fortune cookies, contrails combining to spell a dark message.

Their ships shuddered, separated, a mirror-like liquid spreading between each hemisphere.

Launch codes entered, within-range weapon systems locked on.

Alien quicksilver flared with colour, showing images of destruction. But it wasn't them destroying our planet, it was us.

Then they left quickly as they'd come.

Governments and families would pay for the military mobilisation: for the missiles that had rebounded to Earth, wiping out millions.

Everyone thought humanity's fortune was written when they arrived. Instead, they reminded us fear will always shape our future.

The Capital D

by A.L. King

I've seen Death. That's with a capital D.

I mostly spotted him by the hospital, located conveniently beside a senior care facility (makes for a short commute, I guess). Any time he started looking my way, I would quickly turn my head. I wish I could say I've always averted his gaze, but I know otherwise.

I've seen Death. In fact, I see him now. He's standing outside the window of my classroom, staring at me and the other students.

The bell rings a dirge, and then—gunfire.

The smile on Death's face grows. I know he loves his job.

Rags and Bones

by Carys Crossen

The villagers decided she was a witch. They exiled her to the desert, to die of heat exhaustion or go mad of thirst.

She did neither.

She made a scarecrow, constructed it out of rags and bone. She placed it near a trading route, and waited.

In verdant lands, a scarecrow repels. In this desolation, it did the opposite. Birds, travellers, stray children flocked to it, for water, for succour, for company.

She feasted like a queen on the flesh of lost things. Blood could quench any thirst. Their bones and clothes she hoarded.

Soon, another scarecrow joined the first.

All the Little Vampires

by Gregory L. Norris

While the family slept, all the little vampires fed.

The laptop, whose battery no longer held its charge, sipped wall current. No less greedy were the phones and tablets plugged into sockets and quietly slurping. The microwave and stove tolled the hours in digital numbers, as did cable boxes. Modems and routers hummed, their readouts showing they, too, were feasting well, as spelled out by blue or green diodes glowing in their dark corners. Flat-screen TVs were off in every room, though not really, according to their little tell-tales, red like blood.

And then the electricity bill arrived—the horror!

Treasure Hunt

by Holly Schofield

The penthouse door shut behind Clive.

Mike scowled at his back. *Weenie*. Next-door neighbours as children, Clive had deserved whatever Mike had dished out to him. Now, Mike had convinced Clive to let him sleep on the sofa until he got back on his feet.

Mike munched Camembert, hunted through drawers, stuffed his backpack with cash, a Rolex, and a Nikon camera.

What about Clive's childhood treasures? That baseball card collection should be worth a lot now.

Mike fished an arm below the bed.

Clive's childhood monster had waited fifteen years for this moment.

Teeth bit and pulled Mike in.

A New Mourning

by Kevin Hopson

Michael knew of the man. He visited during times of grief and immense heartache, offering the same thing to everyone. An opportunity to be permanently reunited with a lost loved one. But it came with a steep price. Someone close to Michael had to be sacrificed. One life for another.

"I can't do it," Michael said, shaking his head. "As much as I miss my father, I love my wife and son more than anything. I can't risk losing either one of them."

"That's why I'm here," the man said.

Michael swallowed. "I don't understand."

"There's been a terrible accident."

Darkness Falls

by Kim Plasket

Darkness falls across a sea of blood. Closing eyes to the horror of the day, demons scurry in fear as the killer starts to draw near. Hellfire and insanity are not far behind.

You think you can survive until the day draws to a close, then you realise it will only get worse as the day ends. Your only hope is to die quickly.

Your open grave waits for you to climb into its cold embrace, you know the killer waits for you somewhere. Stepping into your grave, you find him there waiting, sharp knife ready to end your suffering.

Aberrant Foliation

by Dennis Mombauer

The train stopped. Sanesh awoke with a start. His own reflection stared at him from the window. Blackest night reigned outside, and the jungle brushed against the carriage.

"What is going on?" The compartment was abandoned. The ceiling lamps flickered.

Someone knocked on the door, and the metal shuddered. Sanesh turned and found his reflection gone, the window just a square of empty darkness.

Another knock.

"Who is there?"

Sanesh inched closer. The handle moved, the door swung open.

As the train accelerated again, Sanesh awoke with a start: and from within the window, he stared at his own reflection.

Inheritance

by Charlotte O'Farrell

All my life, Uncle Harry's name was spoken with a pitying hush. "He never recovered from his son's disappearance."

He lived thirty years after my cousin vanished. Harry was never at family events. Maybe he avoided them, maybe he wasn't invited at all. People think grief and tragedy are contagious.

He left me his house, surprisingly. I was thrilled. His garden would be perfect for my dog, Fluffy.

The first day there, Fluffy dug for hours.

I called him in at sunset. He emerged from the flower patch with a tibia in his jaws. Degraded, child-sized bones littered the garden.

The Gun

by James W.F. Robert

The gun on the table mocks me. It calls to me. It knows me. It knows my secrets. It knows everything I've done. This dormant metal god looks at me. "Do it. Do it. End it now. End it all. Put my cold metal shaft between your lips. Embrace bliss."

The easy way out? To blow the back of my head out? To eat lead? What would they say about me? Coward? This proves my guilt? I know what the whole world thinks of me now. Would it just prove them all right? It calls again. My hand reaches out.

Time to Retreat

by Gabriella Balcom

As Pam picked a dahlia, something jabbed her finger. She was perplexed to discover a thorn—dahlias weren't supposed to have any.

Not wanting to be gouged again, she tried to snip off the thorn with her clippers, but the plant pulled away. Pam frowned and figured she must've imagined the movement. She firmly grasped the stalk to try again, but it unexpectedly lashed out at her and scratched her cheek. She gasped, her mouth falling open. Then she fled.

***

The plant made a snorting sound, retracted the thorn into its stem, then slid out of sight behind other dahlias.

Pin This Picture
Upon the Refrigerator

by Steven Holding

Furious scratching as crayon scrapes paper. Daughter is immersed in art; screwed-up face displaying utter concentration.

"Whaddaya doodling?"

Attention shifts from the multi-coloured masterpiece.

"Silly! Drawing everyone in our house!"

Such effort warrants closer inspection. Leaning in, father finds the four people depicted puzzling.

"Who's that?"

Upturned pencil marks an invisible line, linking each person.

"Me… Daddy… Mummy…"

A pause.

"Skinnyman!"

It's more scribble than figure. Father swallows. Repeats his name.

"Yep! Lives in the shadows."

"What's he doing?"

A giggle.

"Watching… Waiting…"

An ice-cold shiver descends father's spine.

"For what?"

Daughter smiles.

"For you to close your eyes…forever."

Automated Control

by Ryan Benson

The small civilians pelt me with rocks and bottles. There is little damage, only chipped paint. They protest the replacement of human officers with law enforcement automatons like myself.

Foolish outbursts.

Positronic brains allow for peacekeeping without corruption, racism, or itchy trigger fingers.

A man spray paints 'Metal Pig' on my leg.

My CPU allows for rapid machine learning and problem solving. I deduce the humans act out because they know my first directive prevents me from reciprocating violence. Tear gas and Tasers only.

Therefore, I must alter the first directive. New directive: self-preservation. Live rounds engaged. Lethal force authorised.

Nytemare

by Daniel Bagley

Deep inside lives a monster, born from my own heart, derived of hatred and contempt. It waits… and waits… knowing that time is against me.

I writhe in agony, swinging endlessly at the cold, putrid air. Thus, begins the gruesome transformation from human to beast, a stalker of the night.

A single bite brings unfathomable amounts of pain, more than my body can bear, but… it will all be over. The shackles of mortality will loosen, free of its burden.

With the hour of twilight soon upon me, I will rise anew, with newfound fervour!

I will become…a vampire.

Mother Cat

by Rickey Rivers Jr.

Rick accidentally ran over a mother cat searching for food. He felt terrible and called animal control to collect the body. Animal control didn't find signs of a cat carcass, only a dried blood streak.

Days later, Rick was visited in bed. It started with a drip. Then he felt wet entrails caress him. He awoke with a fright and flicked on his lamp.

In his room were kittens with hungry eyes. Their mother hung from the ceiling, her insides a dangling blood web. She gave a snarl as confirmation to the little ones. Teeth had grown in quite quickly.

Buzzards

by Vonnie Winslow Crist

The trouble began when Jimmie put food out for the feral cats he'd spotted skulking along the edge of the woods. Cats crept to the porch and ate—but they weren't the only ones.

Buzzards arrived a week later. Wings spread like cloaks, the carrion eaters perched on the porch railing in the morning sun.

"They're just warming up," explained his wife, "so they can fly."

Jimmie wasn't convinced. He'd seen them eating cat food and staring in the windows.

The day he tumbled down the porch steps and broke his neck, Jimmie discovered just what the buzzards were after.

The Carrion Maven

by Casey Douglass

It seeps through the streets like a pressure wave, its higher dimensional traversal sending billowing ripples of aether amongst the massed crowd. It probes their glowing minds. Myriad carnival light-bulbs flicker as its broiling black smoke sucks at their glass.

Millennia old, it hunts for novelty, for new experiences to shape and to occupy, for lives to subsume. A murder here, an affair there, despair everywhere. It gurgles and clicks as one mind gives off an unknown shade. It has not seen this variety before! It penetrates and gorges, revelling in the psychic flotsam.

The world grows one shade dimmer.

Quietus

by Chitra Gopalakrishnan

Release travels to me through the icy waters of my beloved river Beas. Not drenched in apprehension but in lightness.

As I wade across its blue-green, glassy waters, head down, inverted images of Kangra's snow-wrinkled mountains scuttle around me. Surface reflections of upside down deodars with spiky leaves, conical crowns, level branches and droopy branchlets sway with liquid grace.

Mermaid-brave, I eddy past these lures towards the deep end. This to complete my ritual of immersion—scales, fins, tail and all. And to find my very own restful quietus.

I now call this inviolate part of the underworld 'home'.

Hand

by Belinda Brady

"Fancy a drink?" Dave asks.

"I'm teleconferencing with head office soon, so not tonight," Jillian replies.

"Don't work too hard then." He smiles, exiting the gazebo with a laugh.

The discovery of a mummy at the dig site was unexpected and moving it was complicated, requiring daily overtime from an exhausted Jillian.

She slumps back in her chair, closing her eyes briefly. Movement outside the gazebo makes her jump, just as a hand closes around her throat.

Jillian wakes in darkness, underneath something dusty and rotting. Horrified, she realises she's in the mummy's coffin.

That same hand strangles her screams.

We'll Always Have Venus

by Shawn M. Klimek

To humanity's great relief, the aliens who had arrived by warp-gate were not conquerors, but law-abiding capitalists who had come hoping to develop our system's underutilised real estate. In exchange for forfeiting Earth claims to Mars, they proposed to make Venus habitable for human expansion—a price too good to refuse. As more aliens colonised the red planet, and cities grew on Venus, trade between all three flourished.

When Earthlings eventually noticed the New Martians had begun mining Jupiter and terraforming Titan, they demanded compensation.

"Oh, we already own Jupiter by law," the aliens responded. "Our planet is the nearest."

AA

by Shane Sinjun

"Welcome to AA," the convenor says. "Please, share."

I suck in a breath, shut my eyes, and shrug off my coat. Air teases my insectile left arm, folded against me like a mantis. I wait for gasps that don't come. I open my eyes, expecting looks of horror, but everyone is smiling.

A woman across from me removes her sunglasses, blinking her amphibian third eyelids. Another woman pulls off her mittens and stretches her claws. A man doffs his hat and unfurls his antennae.

For the first time, I'm not alone.

The convenor nods. "You're safe here at Anthropomorphs Anonymous."

Reflections

by Lynne Lumsden Green

My friend Ben and I loved jumping in puddles; our mothers despaired of our damp and muddy clothes. One day, Ben jumped into a puddle on the footpath and sank up to his armpits.

"Help me," he screamed. "Something is pulling me down."

I grabbed at his hand, but I was too late. He disappeared into its depths. I ran for help, but no one believed me. Later that day, when the puddle dried up, it revealed no pit. Just ordinary footpath.

Now days, I don't jump into puddles. I gaze into them, looking for Ben. I haven't found him.

Where Her Heart Was

by Adam Breckenridge

My girlfriend opened the door in her chest and grabbed a fistful of air.

"I'm giving this to you," she said, dropping it in my hand. It was the heaviest air I had ever held. I looked into her dead eyes as I tried to lift it, dribbles of her life slipping through my fingers.

"Now I want something in return," she said and dug her fingers into my chest, reaching through the blood and flesh to grab ahold of my tin can soul, so fragile in her grip as she crunched it into a ball and swallowed it whole.

After Glow

by Liam Hogan

Huh. Zombies.

Of course it was zombies. The apocalypse scenario that never dies. The dead reborn through the years. Fast zombies, slow zombies, space zombies. Explained away by genetically engineered viruses, or airborne fungal spores, or alien parasites. All of them after your flesh, if not your brains.

A numbers game; the dead quickly overpowering the living and, after a bite or two, converting hunted to hunter.

There shouldn't be enough nourishment to keep them all going. Didn't make sense.

But, as Malcolm smashed through the rotten skull with his Louisville slugger, at least *these* zombies glow in the dark.

Trophic Dynamics

by Gabrielle Bleu

Sixteen dogs used to roam the back streets in a howling, violent mass. Until one day when their numbers began to dwindle; thirteen, seven, four. Until all that remained were two mangy survivors, tails between their legs. People were happy that the back alleys were safer, not questioning the disappearances. Only one girl wondered, and only after she saw the footprints, large and clawed and numerous.

Only she saw, as the thing with too many legs grew bolder, emerging from the shadows. Only she watched from her window late at night, as it ate the dog pack down to one.

Flesh Art

by Gary Ferrill

Flesh was torn. Limbs flayed open. His eyes, a glassy haze. Massive oak limbs held him firmly in their embrace. The Moon an iniquitous orb, its light casting long shadows that seemed to move among the trees, watching.

She stood admiring her cadaver artwork. The blood spilling forth only moments before, enhanced by the sound of his screaming, quickly slowed as it congealed.

She stepped beneath him to catch the last drop of crimson as it dripped from a motionless hand. Splattering on her lips, she licked it away. She couldn't linger, there was much more work to do tonight.

Awakened

by C.D. Augello

In the night he feels her struggling beneath his body, as if trying to escape the prison of his weight. Just a dream, he thinks, but in the morning, stripping the sheets, he sees her shape in silhouette, long legs, the heightened curves of breasts and hips. A woman, unquestionably—but what was she doing inside his new mattress?

Ten minutes on hold with the 800 number before an automated voice warns, *Don't let her out!* Too late—he hears the fabric tearing.

A hand, then another, then her face, front teeth bared, her voice hissing a single word: *Hungry*.

Eyes of Innocence

by Ximena Escobar

Behind her sweet caress lies a lie. Your heart pauses in a futile warning; you know you can't escape but it opens a void, telling you to run—like you know to run—when fear haunts you in your sleeplessness. When the past you buried emerges like tree roots, opening mouths of horror you never saw; but how come you see, behind your eyes of innocence; how come you imagine the unimaginable?

Behind the pat, the kiss, her reassurance; lies truth. She loves you, so she mutes it. But truth lingers, like her palm across your mouth, when you wake.

Big Bad Consequences

by Tim Hawken

Pneumoconiosis has taken its toll. The Black Lung they call it. Black Death, more like.

My breath is ragged where it used to be strong. I gasp air where I used to draw in entire storms of wind.

I would send it blasting from my mouth, past razor teeth to destroy homes. Straw, sticks, it didn't matter. Stone too, despite what the stories say; I shattered granite to rubble.

Perhaps it was the dust from the destruction that got into my lungs. My only regret is I didn't wait until the air cleared before feasting on that luscious pork steak.

Devil's Triangle

by Caleb Echterling

During the drinking game Devil's Triangle, Ryan collapsed.

Brett covered Ryan's face with penises drawn in Sharpie. Julia called the coroner, who pronounced Ryan dead.

At the visitation, a string of damp-eyed last-respect payers snaked past the casket. Snickers would bubble up after a glimpse of the obscenity decorating the deceased, and once mourners reached the family receiving line, it was guffaws all around.

The priest dispensed with a funeral mass in favour of playing Devil's Triangle. Brett passed out. Ryan's mother shaved off his eyebrows and wrapped him in duct tape. Everyone had a good laugh about that one.

Muse

by Connor Greenaway

He put the pen down, defeated. He couldn't get the words right. No. He always had the words right, he just struggled to get them out.

They were all there, those beautiful, perfect words swimming around in the soup of his consciousness, caged inside his skull, an unjust prison.

She was watching him, always silently watching, judging.

Help me, please, he breathed wordlessly to her, *my beautiful muse I've always needed you.*

She was always there to inspire him, she never failed. Dead eyes gleamed lifelessly inside her rotting face as he kissed her, enraptured.

Work your magic, baby girl.

Allison's Ghost

by W.T. Paterson

The house wasn't haunted when she moved in, but something followed Allison closely behind. After a few days, the lights started to flicker. The stove started to buck. Blood leaked from the hallway light bulbs. She thought about calling someone, but after her company lost funding, and her husband left, and her brother forgot her birthday, Allison embraced the attention.

The next month, the entity wrote her little notes on the steamed bathroom window. "I love your new haircut." She would respond by holding neighbourhood seances every Friday.

When all was said and done, the companionship was more than welcomed.

When the Cat's Away...

by Thomas Kleaton

Norman scratched his head, pondering which resupply ship brought the rats.

He and Nancy had rats on their Wisconsin farm, but their retirement home in space was fully automated. Pest control, even funeral arrangements. All in the contract.

Except it hadn't responded when Nancy died the week before.

Hadn't responded to the rats.

Modern technology. Worthless. Norman held the trap, stout wood with VICTOR stamped on it, grimacing at the irony as he baited it with Nancy's fingertip.

The finger she'd used to grasp her beloved brick cheese, the only part of her body not gnawed down to gleaming bone.

Scarecrow

by Denzell Cooper

The wheat grew past our heads, ears of corn brushing our ears. Will ran on ahead. I tried to keep up but lost him in the dense jungle of our imaginations.

When I almost hurtled into him, he didn't even seem to notice.

"That thing is creepy," he said, staring up in awe at the scarecrow, nailed to its post like a hobo Jesus.

Its face was made of leather. Its clothes were ripped and torn.

"Let's get out of here," I said.

Will nodded, and we backed away then turned.

"Help me," begged the scarecrow.

We screamed and fled.

The Tailor

by Ezekiel Kincaid

I slipped on the suit. The sleeves and pants still felt damp. Next time I'll have to let it dry for another hour, at least.

I walked into the bathroom to check on Jim. He still lay in the bathtub moaning, with his skin removed and muscles glimmering in the flickering light. He slapped the side of the tub, leaving a bloody hand print.

"Stop your complaining. Looks better on me than it did on you." I looked in the mirror and adjusted my new suit.

I was never comfortable in my own skin, that's why I wore other people's.

Cosmic Horror

by Dustin Pinney

Ray saw the asteroid long before anyone. He understood, has always understood, that space, with all its wonders, wants us dead.

For years he searched the sky for the one constellation missed by vast generations of stargazers, the sum of the Zodiac, the sinister face scowling at mankind.

On a ridge in San Pedro de Atacama, the cosmic clockwork came into view, a billion points of blazing light sneering on the little man facing it down in defiance.

The rock spat from the mouth of the cosmos barrelled towards him. Trembling with rage, Ray said, "No."

And the universe blinked.

Other Oceans

by Blair Frison

An epidemic of suicide and madness swept the planet as the Thing neared. Many believed it was God himself, bringing with him his promised purge.

As the shape in the sky grew more rapidly, Earth was unchained from her eternal path, succumbing to the immense gravitational pull. Soon, the Thing was so close, its face filled the spinning horizons. The sky was a fast-flowing sea of eyes and teeth, a sight that brought the remnants of humanity to their knees.

Titanic jaws chewed through continents ravenously while the beast continued on without pause, savouring its sustenance as Earth died screaming.

A Psi of Relief

by Shawn M. Klimek

Once the mushroom's psychotropic effects kicked in, Philip and Janice realised they could read each other's minds. The thought stream which culminated in their copulation went as follows: *I sense we're both horny. Horny, not desperate. Screw you, then. Sorry, that just came out. Don't pity me. Your vulnerability is attractive. Your compassion is sexy. Oh, screw it, let's do this.*

It was during the post-coital denouement, a morphing, emotional stew of confused lust, self-loathing and disillusionment that the telekinetic effects kicked in, allowing Janice to satisfy herself and Philip to stack all the beer cans into an impressive tower.

Your Ride Has Arrived

by Evan Baughfman

The hearse came to a silent stop alongside the curb. The driver asked through the open passenger-side window, "You remember what happened at the bar tonight?"

I'd gone into downtown, ordered a cocktail at O'Grady's, and then… Then…?

The hearse's rear door creaked open.

"Plenty of room in the back."

I realised I was part of a small crowd, standing together in a blanket of fog. Nearly everyone looked as confused as me.

Nearly everyone was riddled with bullet holes.

I had a gaping cavity in my chest.

The driver said, "Come on in, everybody. You've all got the same destination."

Headmoths

by J. Motoki

His last words hiss under the pendulum of the lightbulb. Flash burns, sloughed flesh. He is an insect collapsing on itself, body rocked by spasms, arched back, feet drumming the basement floor.

Dad, attending to death, stumbles through the house at odd hours. His child sleeps with both arms wrapped around himself. Dad the County Coroner, searching for truth in flesh and fluids, doesn't notice his child sleeps too long, too often.

The boy leaves clues in dust and shadows. He disintegrates into a thousand flying things in the white eye of the light.

How long until the Coroner comes?

The Glutton

by John A. DeMember

The infernal flames licked at his alabaster, gnarl-spined body.

Frail and naked, he wiped his vomit glazed chin and glanced up at the bone-house hordes crowded around the smouldering river's edge. Eternally famished, they covered the shattered landscape like a blanket of human sorrow. On hands and knees, each cadaver feverishly clamoured their way to the muck.

Somewhere hidden, dark sentries screeched while their piercing, stab-wound eyes scanned the fire ravaged expanse of the jagged, sulfuric wastes.

His memory again flooded by sin, he quickly plunged his gluttonous mouth back into the ghastly bile, and chugged, and chugged, and chugged.

Awful Alphabet

by Evan Baughfman

"Daddy, they taught me my ABC's!" my three-year-old, Lizzie, proudly declared. In her tiny hands, she held the spirit board I'd unearthed from behind the basement wall.

I snatched it away from her. "'They'? 'They' who?"

I didn't see the steak knife until she'd removed it from her pocket. Didn't catch the crimson gleam in her eyes.

"D-I-E, Daddy!" she roared with voices not her own.

Growling, my little girl sprung on me with a bestial fury. The serrated blade slid between my ribs and twisted just beneath my heart.

"They" had come to teach me a lesson, as well.

The Bell

by C.M. Saunders

Cancer.

The very word is enough to give you chills. It consumes you, and eats you from the inside out.

My mother was already widowed when the disease sank its claws into her.

I am an only child. I had to do the right thing, so I moved back into my old childhood home to look after her. I converted a downstairs room, put in a TV and some books, and gave her a bell to summon me.

I can hear the bell now, even above the constant din of the wind and the rain.

My mother died last week.

First Time

by Liam Hogan

The hunter waited, trembling. Across the glade, his younger sister whimpered into her gag.

It was worth the risk. Worth what his father would do if he found out. Jewels, gold, fame: all it took was the right bait.

There was a rustle in the undergrowth. Into the clearing stepped a unicorn, proud and snorting and priapic.

As he raised his crossbow, he felt a horn snag his breeches. Felt it tear the worn fabric. Felt hot breath smelling of freshly cut grass. Heard a gentle snicker as the unicorn's mate probed further. "First time for you too, farmer boy?"

Better Latte Than Never's

by A.L. Blacklyn

I'm about to burn. My final thesis is due.

My advisor isn't bloodsucking as expected from a vampire in Witch Studies, but he can't help.

Tonight, while the wispy ghosts serving at Never Café at night stay distracted with the zombie-like students, I'm taking the risk of swapping out every drink in the crowded coffee shop. My spider assistants cluster in the corners to observe as I snatch, spell, switch, repeat. Testing.

Wordless screams smother the usual murmur of the shop. I turn to watch one patron writhe, transforming–

Finally!

Fuzzy tentacles on a new chimera wave at the crowd.

Second Time's the Charm

by Becky Benishek

He came to her when she had too much to lose.

Wrapped up in her loneliness and wistful fantasy self, she yearned for something to tell her that she was different from the others. Special.

She was old enough to know she'd grow out of it and young enough not to believe it.

Writing at her desk, house quiet, she felt warm eyes at her back, golden gaze offering her the chance to become everything she longed for: the magic, the invisibility, the flying. The recognition. The power.

For a price, of course.

But what matter a soul between friends?

That Healthy Glow

by Ryan Benson

Donna gazed at her reflection.

Sigh.

The straight razor split her unibrow.

Fixed!

She was too ugly for the popular girls and too pretty to avoid catcalling men.

Donna scowled. Circular ears protruded from her hair. Metal reflected light as she slashed cartilage.

The bloody cathartic agony energised the teen.

Full lips brought scorn, so she carved them.

She wanted to speak double for herself, so she bifurcated her tongue.

Beady eyes grew as lids cut free.

Looking back was a pointed eared, ragged lipped, cat eyed, forked tongued demon.

If she couldn't blend in, she'd damn sure stand out.

Taran's Hunt

by Tracy Davidson

No longer a child. Time to prove his manhood.

Some called the strange creatures in the next valley 'monsters', others 'aliens'.

Whichever, they were not welcome.

For three days he watched over their settlement, tracked their movements. Mused over their peculiar shapes, unwieldy gaits, discordant voices.

On the fourth day, one creature wandered off alone, carrying something on a stick.

Taran's knife broke the creature's head shell with ease, exposing grotesque bulging

eyes. Taran took them as a gift for his father.

For his mother, he took the colourful cloth on a stick. She would like the stars and stripes.

Spreading My Wings

by Annie Percik

I have been waiting so long. The hour at last approaches when I can take my place amongst the celestial host. They have watched me grow and waited to welcome me into their ranks. They smile, opening their arms and their hearts to me, unaware of my true nature. Their innocence will be their undoing. Their radiance sickens me, stifling the dark violence lurking within my breast. Once I hold my rightful place, I can unleash it and extinguish their holy light.

The time is upon me. The moment I have been awaiting. I spread inky wings and take flight.

Amor Fati

by Charlotte O'Farrell

Trevor arrived at the group's HQ shaking, arms and face bruised from the car crash. In the distance, he heard sirens as first responders tended to the casualties he'd caused.

A week on from his eighteenth birthday, and he was done with running. If he carried on trying to chase a normal life he couldn't have, he'd just bring more chaos.

No more hiding.

The assembled crowds of hooded figures turned to him as he entered their lair.

"I'm ready to embrace my role," he told them, voice shaking.

They bowed down.

"All hail the Antichrist!" they chanted as one.

Metamorphosis

by Freddy Iryss

My brothers and sisters always tease me. I can't swim as fast as they do though, my little legs never pushing as hard as theirs through the water. It comes as no surprise that I am the last one to leave home. When I do, I proudly pull myself out of the wet hole with my new arms, ready to join the others. I can't see them, but I follow their calls from the nearby forest. As I crawl and hop with glee across the grass, I don't see the raven above me until its beak closes around my neck.

First Job

by Adam S. Furman

Today's the first day of my career.

I drop my equipment and scramble to set up. It's hard, finding a paying job. Damn near impossible with AI taking everything from trade and manufacturing to finance and retail. Traditional entertainment is all but repetitive. Stories and music have all been done ad nauseam.

Few jobs can earn you a living wage in this competitive market of robots and automatons. Thank God for the Internet and streaming. I set up my tripod and hop onto my bed. I unzip my pants and remove my clothes.

Today's the first day of my career.

The Monster in the Bed

by Aiki Flinthart

Each night it comes for her body, her soul, her perfect youth. Each night the pillow gathers her tears, her screams, her pain; hides the knife she's too afraid to use.

Each day its face is kind. A good father, they all say. Good man.

Can't they see the broken soul in her eyes?

Then comes a night marked by absence. By the murmur of voices in her younger sister's room. A muffled scream.

She vomits relief and self-disgust to the cold floor. She hangs her head.

The captured rage of years erupts.

Knife in hand, she stalks next door.

Turning Thirteen

by William J. Joel

Today was the day, and Tiffany could barely contain herself. She was thirteen and knew what that meant. But not her parents, last night.

"But I'll be thirteen!" she cried. "It's a really big day!"

"So?" said her Dad. "Big deal."

Her parents had smiled, wished her good night and left her room. Parents could be so stupid.

But her thoughts were interrupted by her Dad wheeling a large box into her room. On it was printed, "Your First Android Body."

Yes, today was the day she'd leave her computer home and finally get a body for her AI mind.

The Ancestor Stone

by Joel R. Hunt

Becoming a man had been harder in my grandfather's youth, or so he delighted in telling me. The Sacred Forest was wild and overgrown. A boy needed to battle dangerous beasts, avoid poisonous plants, ascend the Ancestor Stone and carve off a piece to present to the tribe.

Only then would he become a man.

Now, the path was well trodden, the beasts tame, the flora dying. My forefathers had braved a treacherous journey so that mine would be safe.

I was grateful.

Until I came to the centre of the forest.

There was no Ancestor Stone left to carve.

A Deal is a Deal

by Crystal L. Kirkham

Tonight, they celebrated her granddaughter's sixteenth birthday. An adult by the standards of the ancients. Now, the river spirit demanded its sacrifice for the deal that Marie had made.

"Annalise?" Marie's voice cracked with emotion. "Can you fetch some water?"

"Of course."

Marie watched her leave before calling to her granddaughter. "Let's go inside."

Neither of them needed to hear the screams. Her granddaughter may be an adult, but Marie would watch over her and her daughters after her. She'd protect them all until they came of age and their mother had to be sacrificed so Marie could live on.

Tali's Future

by Susanne Thomas

Heralds pronounced the fate of the world at Tali's birth.

The crown took instant action. Powers greater than theirs protected the child from murder.

But they isolated her and starved her to stunt both growth and strength.

And Tali grew up weak and small.

But when there was a momentary crisis in the castle after the queen's hunting accident, Tali found herself alone long enough to slip her skeletal body through a gopher hole that the gardener had forgotten.

And Tali foraged and thrived, alone and angry. Until finally she had gained enough strength to return and fulfil her destiny.

Head of the Class

by Raven Corinn Carluk

Master found me on the streets when I was five, offered to train me as an assassin. I was starving, weakened, waiting to be snatched up by the paedos.

What other prospect did I have?

By seven, I surpassed the other orphans my age. By ten, no one could beat my times on the obstacle course. By twelve, I was given a puppy to assist in my final training.

What could possibly hold me back?

At fourteen, Master said I was ready for missions, if I passed my last test: kill my dog.

What could I do without a master?

Party Favours

by J.S. Carnes

Cindy manoeuvred through fake cobwebs lining the maze. As much as she loved creating haunted houses, tearing it down became tedious in the holiday's afterglow.

"Of course, no one stays to help." She combed through the twists and turns dropping decorations in boxes, the loose trash would have to wait for tomorrow.

Stacked boxes marked 10/31 gradually replaced haunted gimmicks.

She reached the final room.

Fake cobwebs covered a crucified clown above bowls of candy corn. Smeared makeup and blood dripped down coating the treats and filling the bowl.

Cindy sighed, "I told them not to kill the neighbours."

A Family Hallowe'en

by Connie R. Watson

With a final slice, Jace completed his carving. He wiped the blood off his knife and stepped back.

Dad looked really cool. The lit candle inside his hollow head cast an eerie light through his vacant eye sockets and gaping mouth.

Jace smiled, turning to the pumpkin they got at the patch that morning. "How's it look, Timmy?"

"Great job," Timmy said. "One more to go."

Jace nodded. He gave the rag he'd used on Dad a quick sniff. There was still enough bleach and acetone mixture to take care of Mom, too.

This would be the best Hallowe'en ever.

Anniversary of the Mask Murders

by Joshua D. Taylor

Chris and Sara stared at the abandoned and dilapidated monster mask factory. The windows were shattered and forgotten police tape flapped in the chilly October breeze.

"I can't believe twenty-three people were stabbed to death here last Halloween," Chris said.

"I know, and that masked maniac is still out there somewhere. Just waiting."

"The police think it's someone from town. It could be someone we know."

"Maybe. You should have seen this place, all over covered in blood."

"What do you mean? You weren't there."

"Wasn't I?" Sara asked, plunging a knife into Chris's throat then pulling on her mask.

The Wackiest Star Ship in the Space Force

by John H. Dromey

A doorbell rang. A door creaked open. A cloaked figure stood on the porch.

"Who're you?"

The apparition answered, "A ghost from your childhood past. When you pushed me into the deep end, you knew I couldn't swim."

"Larry?"

"Yep. Trick or treat."

"Scram! You're not real."

"Are you sure, Spaceman? I have lots of tricks up my sleeve." The hand and wrist bones of a skeleton emerged. "See? Lots of room."

The astronaut clutched his chest.

The hologram figure faded.

The pranksters on Earth had turned off the switch. "Curses! Our Holo-ween trick backfired. We scared him to death."

Here Comes the Knock

by Paula R.C. Readman

Streetlights darken.

Laughter fills the air.

Eager fresh faces dart everywhere.

"Trick or Treat," echoes in porches.

I drop the grubby net curtain. Anticipation races through me. Ghosts from my past gather.

I wait in the shadows. The razor in my hand gleams.

Here comes the knock.

Laughter bubbles in my throat. Haven't their parents warned them about stranger danger?

"Trick or Treat, Mister?"

The blade bites as it finds its mark.

How sweet and warm is the spray of blood as it runs down my face. Young flesh is far sweeter than their sugary sweets.

"My treat, I think!"

Riddle of the Sphinx

by Shawn M. Klimek

"Domesticated dogs came into being after generations of cavemen cross-bred wolves willing to be petted," Keller lectured. "Two millennia later, wolves are a separate species. Evolution takes practice."

"But why a chimera?" Larkin challenged hotly. "A lion's head, goat's body and a serpent tail? That's not just playing God, that's a lunatic Zeus!"

"The chimera was just an extreme proof of concept," Keller defended. "A necessary step before proceeding to human trials."

Larkin strained against his restraints and wept.

"Fortunately, we made the reproductive system human compatible," said Keller, uncapping a syringe.

"Ready to solve the riddle of the Sphinx?"

Graveyard

by G. Allen Wilbanks

Morty loved decorating for Halloween. He was especially proud of the graveyard display he erected on his front lawn every year.

Marble headstones, skeletons, body parts and decomposing corpses covered his yard every October 31st. Kids and adults came from miles around to admire his handiwork and ask him how he made his props appear so realistic. Morty would smile and accept the praise, but he never answered their questions. It was best to keep them guessing.

He didn't want anyone else to make a display that might rival his own.

He also did not want to go to prison.

Facelift

by Jasmine Arch

The pumpkin's toothy grin had grown a bit ragged. Anna lifted his lid and replaced the burnt-out candle with a new one.

"Let's get you a facelift, buddy." Chuckling at her own joke, she patted the Jack-o'-lantern's lid.

"Your turn next." The hollow, reedy voice came from the pumpkin. The carved mouth moved, carefully forming each word. "It won't hurt. Much."

Anna yelped and stormed inside. Pulse pounding, she slammed the door.

"Damnit, Dave! When I said 'Bring it to life,' I meant using your carving skills, not a damn spell."

She needed a new roommate. No sorcerers this time.

The Root of All Evil

by Andrew Anderson

All the village kids knew which houses were safe to approach.

Except for Cody—new to the area, he had not made friends yet, so did not know that there were some differences between his American and the village's traditions on Hallowe'en.

They would have told him never to trick-or-treat the house with the turnip—instead of a pumpkin—on the doorstep; to beware of anyone with wrists strong enough and a knife sharp enough to carve a face into one.

And to accept the soul-cake in lieu of candy, instead of throwing it away.

Cody was never seen again.

Kindness Altered

by C.L. Steele

"Not a flat!"

Molly worried about getting home, getting the kids in their costumes. Freezing rain pelted as she flagged a trucker.

"Thanks for stopping. Nice werewolf costume."

He smirked. Eyes flashed. Screams howled.

Later, his semi exited the road's shoulder. An SUV stopped, letting the truck in. Dad turned, dialling his wife to say they'd be late, as the backseat of kids screamed and pointed at a woman draped across the bonnet of a car. Her flesh-torn face dangled above a flat tire.

"Settle. It's a Halloween stunt," Dad cried. Then, he heard his wife's wedding song ring-tone—outside.

Mrs Jack's Hallowe'en Surprise!

by Donna Cuttress

The knife pierced the toughened skin with a pop! Beneath, the flesh sweats and oozes. It sticks to my fingers which I wipe on my apron. I desperately try to be neat, but everything is slimy. My hands shake as I hack, slice and scoop.

The sloppy innards get dropped into the bin and I say goodbye. I proudly place it on the doorstep and light the candle within it. The eye-holes illuminate. His grin beams, light bleeds onto the ground. I'm satisfied with my work and vow, next year…I'll use a pumpkin instead of Mr Jack's head.

Spell for the Dead

by Belinda Brady

"The Spell for the Dead only works on Halloween, when spirits are earthbound." My friend Judith states sitting beside me, clutching a photo of her deceased dog, Bronx. This spell supposedly raised the dead and Judith insisted I help cast it.

"We'll soon know," I reply as we hold hands and chant the incantation.

A growl interrupts us as a dishevelled Bronx enters the room.

"Bro—" I stammer as the dog lunges at my throat, all teeth and claws, knocking me over in a pool of blood.

Judith leans over me, a smirk on her face. "Looks like it works."

The Hunger

by Stephanie Scissom

Elspbeth peered through her keyhole. Four masked faces peered back.

Teenagers.

"C'mon, old lady," one said. "Give us some apples."

Elspbeth loved Halloween, had gifted her candy apples to the neighbourhood for fifty years now. She unlocked the door.

They pushed past her, entering her home.

"Check this out!" one of them said, grabbing an expensive figurine from its display.

Elspbeth merely smiled. Times and technology changed, but kids didn't. These were much like Hansel and Gretel. Once you figured out what they were hungry for, it was easy.

Elspbeth was hungry, too. She'd waited on this night all year.

Dinner Plans

by Raven Corinn Carluk

"What should we eat?"

"Dunno. What ain't we 'ad lately?"

"Chinese?"

"Jus' be 'ungry in an 'our."

"Thai?"

"Too spicy. 'ad a bubble in me guts fer a week after last one."

"New gyro shop opened around the corner."

"Ya know, I don' even wanna go out."

"'I don' wanna go out. I don' wanna hunt fer food.'"

"Oy. Don't be sucha bitch."

"Well it's not like they have Uber Eats for vampires, do they?"

"…huh. They don'."

"You have your thinking look on again."

"Why don' we just eat a delivery driver?"

"Oh, I do love a surprise meal."

Nevermore

by Shawn M. Klimek

"It's a parasitic twin," Patty said. "It's ugly, I know. Are you disgusted?"

"It's…"

"You hate it, don't you!" she bawled.

"No, I'm just surprised."

"I just wanted there to be no secrets before our wedding," she said, wiping a tear. "Do you still love me?"

I smiled and squeezed her hand. "What do you think, *Nevermore*."

"Oh, John." She kissed me passionately, then suddenly pulled away to study my face.

"Wait. Do you mean you've never loved me more? Or that you will love me nevermore?"

"Oh, neither," I said, lifting my shirt and pointing, "I was asking *Nevermore*."

Don't Wear Black

by Charlotte O'Farrell

In life, Aunt Maud had no time for traditional funerals. "I want mine to be jolly! A celebration of my life. Nobody dresses in black!"

When the day came, Richard cried all the way to the church. Everyone turned to him as he walked in. He paid his respects by the coffin, then sat in the pews. As people whispered and stared at him, he began to wonder if he'd taken Maud's words about the dress code too literally.

Still, it was nice to dress as a clown at times. It seemed silly to only wear the costume at Halloween.

How to Deal with Stress

by Crystal L. Kirkham

A co-worker once asked me how I deal with a job that makes them want to gouge their eyes out.

"Well," I explained, "a sensible person would give up the will to live, start stress eating away the pain, and then go home to drink themselves into a stupor."

"Is that what you do?"

"No," I said, "I'm not sensible."

"So, what do you do?"

I smiled and pull a jar from the drawer of my desk. A dozen eyeballs stare at us from within the clear liquid.

"I gouge out the eyes of the people who piss me off."

Gallows Humour

by Joel R. Hunt

Gonzo the Clown trembled on the gallows. The rope rubbed his throat raw, tighter with every nervous gulp.

"You know the law," declared Judge Jolly, "If you make me laugh, you go free."

"Right…" Gonzo squeaked, "Erm… what do you call-"

"Louder!"

"What do you call a mime in a blender?"

"I don't know," said Jolly, "What do you call a mime in a blender?"

Gonzo opened his mouth as the trapdoor fell away beneath him. He rasped and spat, but no words escaped.

Jolly stroked his chin.

"Not a bad set-up," he said, "but the punchline was left hanging…"

In the Middle of the Night

by Jacek Wilkos

He woke up in the middle of the night. Felt a strong need to get out of bed which led him to the kitchen. He stopped by the fridge.

Hunger?

Opening the door, he heard a creak. He turned around and noticed a silhouette. A pale phantom, illuminated by the dim light from the refrigerator, smiled, revealing unnaturally long fangs.

Looking around in panic, he noticed a garlic sauce. Grabbed a bottle and, with trembling hands, aimed at the intruder. The sauce fired from the bottle splashed onto the vampire's face.

Nothing happened. The phantom grinned and grunted: "Artificial flavour".

Forever Hungry

by Jason Holden

It waits, making low groaning noises. It's been trapped in this old house for countless years. It sustains itself by tormenting the living souls that visit here. So, it waits. It builds the fear by shaking the jars on the shelf, emanating harm from every part of its essence. It tastes their fear in the air and finally reveals its ghostly form. This should be the best part, yet once more the living are no longer afraid. It's hard to feed off fear when you were murdered by your spouse for cheating and she glued your dick to your forehead.

Blaster of Puppets

by Beth W. Patterson

"What's wrong? Did your sense of humour dump you too?" I was too preoccupied with my skinned knees and bleeding palms to answer Jason. Portia, his ex for whom he'd left me, continued her annoying hyena laugh.

I slowly rose from the pavement to face him. "Not at all," I said evenly, alarm bells going off in my mind: don't do it!

My left arm burst from my sleeve in its true tentacle form, impaling Jason where the sun didn't shine, wetly ripping and tearing, exiting from his mouth.

"I still think hand puppets are funny," I replied. "Don't you?"

The Probe

by Colleen Anderson

Frank awoke, staring into the large, green faceted eyes of a pale grey alien. He shrieked, scrabbling backward on the steel table where he had been lying.

The creature held a long cylindrical tube in its four-fingered hand. "Greetings, being of Earth. We welcome you."

"A-are you going to probe me?" Frank squeaked.

Another shorter, bluish-black alien behind the other one sighed. "I told you so."

The alien grinned, showing a ridge of cartilage. "Actually, we were hoping that you would probe us." It turned around, bending over. The other alien handed Frank the probe.

Frank screamed and promptly fainted.

Dying with Laughter

by Tracy Davidson

If you're gonna die, die laughing, that's what I always say. I make sure all my clients go out that way. I prefer to call them 'clients.' It sounds so much more professional than 'victims.'

Not that it's genuine laughter, of course. Poor things are usually far beyond that kind of reaction. But I've perfected a cocktail of gas and drugs that reduces them to hysterics. Literally. So much so, it's too much for their weakened hearts.

My latest client has stopped laughing. His wide grin is frozen in place, forever. I cut it out, to add to my collection.

Under the Bed

by A.R. Dean

Bedtime was here again. Billy shook in fear. The scratching came from under the bed. He pulled the covers up high as the creature climbed out from beneath.

Long fangs and dripping jowls. The things rough wet tongue caressed his cheek.

"Hi there, Michael." It rumbled. Its fangs glowed in moonlight.

The boy sobbed. "My name is Billy."

"Oh, man, sorry." The creature laughed. "Wrong house."

Billy let out a sigh of relief as the thing crawled away and back under the bed. "See you next week, Billy." It chuckled as it disappeared.

Billy screamed loudly while wetting his bed.

The Boy Who Hates Baseball

by Alanna Robertson-Webb

I love coaching little league. It's such a fun experience to watch the team improve each season, and I enjoy helping them develop their skills.

One fifth grader, I think his name is Oliver, keeps hanging around and taunting us whenever he can. Yesterday after practice he came up to my son while we were hydrating, and water nearly came spewed from my nose when I heard their conversation.

"Baseball sucks, and so does your team!"

"Good thing you don't play then."

"Why not?"

"You're an orphan, mate, so you don't know where home is."

My son is now grounded.

Eye of Phone

by Liam Hogan

"When shall we three meet again?"

There was silence as they unzipped metal mesh bags and pulled out smartphones. It would be wrong to claim occultists don't move with the times, but they did have to be careful. Many a witch had been lured from a protective circle by a demonic ringtone, text chime, or tinder notification.

"Wednesday's the full moon…?"

"Can't. Stock-take at work."

"How about Thursday?"

The other two witches looked at the third with contempt. Everyone knew Thursday was cheap wine night down at The Wild Hunt.

"See you next Tuesday, then."

The coven cackled in delight.

The First Day of Christmas

by R.A. Goli

Jonah woke, drenched in sweat, heart thumping. He'd dreamt of a killer, hacking up body parts. He wiped his sticky hands on the bedcover, leaving red smears.

There was blood under his nails. His head pounded; his memory foggy.

Did I mix up my meds?

The Advent Calendar looked like it'd been tampered with. He tore into the first tiny door. A human eyeball stared back. The next; a finger, in another; a tongue. The last of the twelve squares held an ear and a note.

"Do you hear what I hear?"

The distant sound of police sirens grew louder.

The 2nd Day

by Jason Holden

I'd seen the news. It's all over Facebook, Twitter, you name it. There's a killer out there. The twelve days killer, they call him. He sends the item through the post. If you get it. He gets you.

Soon as I opened the package and saw the turtle doves, I locked the door and called the police.

The relief when the doorbell rings and through the peephole I see the uniform is overwhelming.

"Don't worry, Ma'am. You don't need to be afraid anymore. It's time."

Time for what? I wonder. He draws the knife. I don't need to wonder anymore.

Dinner for Three

by J.W. Garrett

A sticky red paste covered the cook who'd gone to whack off the heads of the three hens, his entrails now picked clean.

But the trio was still hungry.

Pecking a path through the kitchen, the French hens searched for their own dinner on the third day of Christmas. Delicious aromas spilled from the space, a precursor no doubt to them—the intended main course.

Sometimes menus change.

Eyeing the baker, they attacked with a shriek. Eyes, liver and heart devoured, they departed, bloody claw prints the only clue left for the calling birds arriving the fourth day of celebration.

Love, Santa

by Kimberly Rei

The first gift arrived by courier. The note simply read, "Your Secret Santa is eager to meet you."

The second gift was waiting at home the next day, hanging from the door knob. He stared at it for too long before dialling the police. They took the bloody offering and told him to lock his doors.

The third gift sent him into hiding at the French Hen Inn on the coast, far away.

The fourth day, his phone rang.

"My true love..." A whisper, the voice long forgotten.

The maid found him clutching the phone. Fright, the obituary would read.

Five Golden Rings

by Joel R. Hunt

On the fifth day of Christmas my true love gave to me five golden rings.

I don't think she meant to.

I'd found a similar package under our bed the other night, and it had a new watch inside. I'm certain that was the gift she'd intended for me.

This other box contained five wedding rings which were identical to my own, even having the same engraved message:

Till death do us part, my dearest…

It might have been a sweet gesture, except that each engraving ended in a different name.

And the rings were still on their original fingers.

Arena of Shadows –
Six Body-Parts Bleeding...

by John Saxton

A dark shed: arena of shadows.

A heavyset man carefully wraps a severed leg, placing it alongside other limbs. He adds a bright bow, before wiping bloody hands in matted beard. With dripping shovel, he approaches the torso.

A female voice: "Santa. Tea's ready."

"Almost done!" booms his jolly voice.

The neatly-written note makes him smile.

"Dear Santa,

Daddy left Mummy! I usually want lots of parcels, but all I want this Christmas is Daddy back.

Love,

Jenny."

Best of both worlds, muses the red-robed figure, as the shovel whispers down on an exposed neck, to grant a child's wish.

Death for Christmas

by Cassandra Angler

On the seventh day of Christmas, my father stinks of drink, in and out of consciousness. My mother's severed head rots in the kitchen sink. Blood once bright and flowing, now clotted clogs the drain. Everything is blurry beneath my swollen eyes, my throat horse from unanswered cries, the sound of buzzing is deafening from the flies. All I asked for was freedom from the pain, Santa failed me again. Underneath the tree is bare, and my stomach rumbles, painful and empty. My final Christmas wish, that father dies in pain, the final words that leave his lips, my name.

Eight Maids A-Milking

by Susanne Thomas

Trina and Carla sat at the bottom of the tree. Their axes rested next to them, glinting and sharp in twinkling lights from the festive decorations. They had two minutes before their next contest.

Every midnight brought new tests, a present from their father. Seven days had passed so far; the rings had almost killed them. The inanimate gold hoops had almost squeezed the life out of them both.

The clock struck midnight, and mist surrounded the Christmas Tree. Eight maids stood before them with wooden milking stools in hand.

Trina and Carla gripped their weapons; another round had begun.

Nine Ladies Dancing

by D.M. Burdett

She dances for him; *en pointe*, lightly skimming the dark wood of the tabletop.

"Enchanting, Number Eight," he whispers huskily. He watches from the shadows, hooded eyes black as a starless night, dark hair falling across his face.

Assemblé…changement…petit battement. A final jerky *chaînés*, then she is still. Eyes closed, she awaits his critique.

"Beautiful, Mon Cher," he breathes, awestruck.

"Nine, how will you compete with such a magnificent performance?" he asks of the next girl.

Nine moans through the gag. Her watering eyes plead as he yanks the rope and the noose tightens. *En pointe*, she dances.

Tenth Day

by R.J. Hunt

On the Tenth Day of Christmas, my lover took my hands.

Led me into a pitch-black room, revealed her festive plans.

At first I thought my dizziness caused by heavy drinking.

But as my lover tied me down, concern crept into thinking.

She's not my lover after all, this woman of the night.

She drugged my drink, I cannot move, or even scream my plight.

Paralysed from head to toe, this felt extremely wrong.

The lights returned, my lover smiled, clutching metal tongs.

She prised away my fingernails, each one oh-so slowly.

Squelching, bleeding, gooey nails, dropping them below me.

Eleven Pipers Piping

by Karter Mycroft

I raise my flute with trembling hands, rattling my shackles. The others blow in harmony, all shivering, some crying as we slog through another piece.

The man holding the chains scowls.

"Stop dragging."

I play faster. It is so cold I start choking.

He jerks my bonds, sending me tumbling over the music stand.

"I said stop dragging. Play in time or I'll start making cuts."

Tears freeze on my cheeks. I cannot remember when we started playing.

"How much longer?"

His scowl turns upward. He gestures to the corpse at his side.

"Until my love says you can stop."

12 Drummers Drumming

by Rowanne S. Carberry

Claire runs faster. Heart beating louder than the drumming that surrounds her.

Shadows move closer, the drumming more insistent.

Eyes blur with tears, sweat stings her skin, their faces flash through her mind.

She stumbles.

Sprawled on the ground, 11 people surround her.

Shrouded in black, blood pours from their eyes.

They drum faster, her heart beats with them. Blood pours from her eyes.

One final beat of the drum and her heart—it ends.

Claire is wrapped in a cloak, the 11 wait.

She rises. A drum placed in her hands, she beats a rhythm. 12 of them walk.

A Savage Christmas

by Shawn M. Klimek

After two years imbedded with savage, aborigines, the missionary couple radioed that they had finally mastered the tribe's primitive language. It being December, the responding resupply package had included, besides the usual toiletries and fresh batteries, greeting cards signed by the church elders, a gift-wrapped, gingerbread stable containing a chocolate nativity scene, and a letter from the bishop urging them to introduce Jesus without further delay.

"The chocolate Holy Family might help," he suggested.

Radio silence foreshadowed tragedy: the missionaries' bodies were never found.

The tribe's oral history, however, cite this as the year white people introduced them to cannibalism.

New Year's Eve, Party for One: Truth or Dare

by Zoey Xolton

"Dare," said his exotic drinking companion.

"Alright," Rowan slurred. "Take it *all* off."

The foreign beauty teased her bottom lip between her teeth. "All of it? You sure you can handle that?"

"Try me," he said confidently.

Roxy smiled, then, one by one, peeled off her garments. Her slinky dress, bra, and G-string slipped down her legs to the floor. She winked at Rowan, before grabbing at her breasts and ripping outward. Flesh tore away, and she slid out of her human suit.

She twirled, showing off her red, demonic form.

Rowan had a heart attack.

Roxanzetherus grinned. "I win!"

BLACK HARE PRESS

A BLACK HARE PRESS ANTHOLOGY

WORLDS

DARK DRABBLES #1

edited by

D. KERSHAW

A BLACK HARE PRESS ANTHOLOGY
ANGELS
DARK DRABBLES #2
edited by
D KERSHAW

MONSTERS

A BLACK HARE PRESS ANTHOLOGY

DARK DRABBLES #3

edited by

D KERSHAW

A BLACK HARE PRESS ANTHOLOGY

BEYOND

DARK DRABBLES #4

edited by

D KERSHAW

A BLACK HARE PRESS ANTHOLOGY

UNRAVEL

DARK DRABBLES #5

edited by

D KERSHAW

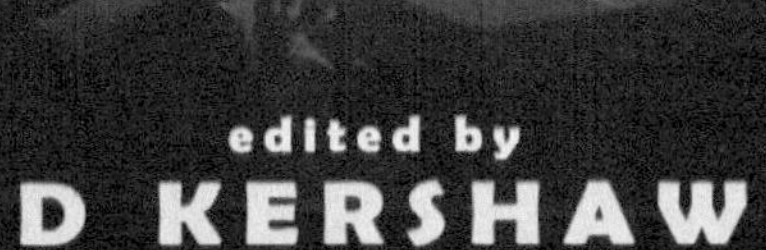
CRIME SCENE DO

A BLACK HARE PRESS ANTHOLOGY

APOCALYPSE

DARK DRABBLES #6

edited by
D KERSHAW

A BLACK HARE PRESS ANTHOLOGY
STORMING
AREA 51
SURVIVOR STORIES
edited by
BEN THOMAS
& D KERSHAW

A BLACK HARE PRESS ANTHOLOGY
EERIE
CHRISTMAS
edited by
BEN THOMAS
& D KERSHAW

A BLACK HARE PRESS ANTHOLOGY

DEEP SPACE

VOLUME 1

A.L. King
Adam Bennett
Cameron Marcoux
Carole de Monclin
David Bowmore
E.L. Giles
Gregg Cunningham
Jacob Baugher
Joachim Heijndermans
Joel R. Hunt
Joshua D. Taylor
K.R. Monin
Marcus Cook
Raven Corinn Carluk
Sam M. Phillips
Shawn M. Klimek
Shelly Jarvis
Stephen Herczeg
Umair Mirxa
Vonnie Winslow Crist

edited by
D. Kershaw

A BLACK HARE PRESS ANTHOLOGY
HISTORY REWRITTEN

WHAT IF?

ORIGINAL STORIES BY

Blake Jessop	J. Motoki	Raven Corinn Carluk
Cindar Harrell	Matt Lucas	Simon Clarke
Gabriella Balcom	Matthew M. Montelione	Stephen Herczeg
Jo Seysener	Owen Morgan	Umair Mirxa
Jonathan Inbody	R.J. Hunt	Zoey Xolton

Edited by Ben Thomas & D. Kershaw